The Best Gift

Level 1D

Written by Anne Marie Ryan
Illustrated by Florencia Denis
Reading Consultant: Betty Franchi

About Phonics

Spoken English uses more than 40 speech sounds.
Each sound is called a *phoneme*. Some phonemes relate
to a single letter (d-o-g) and others to combinations
of letters (sh-ar-p). When a phoneme is written down,
it is called a *grapheme*. Teaching these sounds, matching
them to their written form, and sounding out words for
reading is the basis of phonics.

Early phonics instruction gives children the tools to sound
out, blend, and say the words without having to rely on
memory or guesswork. This instruction gives children the
confidence and ability to read unfamiliar words, helping
them progress toward independent reading.

About the Consultant

Betty Franchi is an American educator with a Bachelor's Degree in Elementary and Middle Education as well as a Master's Degree in Special Education. Betty holds a National Boards for Professional Teaching Standards certification. Throughout her 24 years as a teacher, she has studied and developed an expertise in Phonetic Awareness and has implemented phonetic strategies, teaching many young children to read, including students with special needs.

Reading tips

This book focuses on consonant, vowel, consonant, consonant words.

Tricky and/or new words in this book

Any words in bold may have unusual spellings or are new and have not yet been introduced.

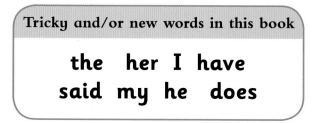

Tricky and/or new words in this book

**the her I have
said my he does**

Extra ways to have fun with this book

After the readers have finished the story, ask them questions about what they have just read.

What test does Bess set?
Who wins the test?

Make flashcards for each of the sounds within the pronunciation guide. This will help reinforce letter/ sound matches.

I am a princess and I have lots of books. I sit on my throne to read. The Queen listens and says, "Bravo!"

A Pronunciation Guide

This grid highlights the sounds used in the story and offers a guide on how to say them.

s	a	t	p
as in sat	as in ant	as in tin	as in pig
i	n	c	e
as ink	as in net	as in cat	as in egg
h	r	m	d
as in hen	as in rat	as in mug	as in dog
g	o	u	l
as in get	as in ox	as in up	as in log
f	b	j	v
as in fan	as in bag	as in jug	as in van
w	z	y	k
as in wet	as in zip	as in yet	as in kit
qu	x	ff	ll
as in quiz	as in box	as in off	as in fill
ss	zz	ck	
as in hiss	as in buzz	as in duck	

Be careful not to add an /uh/ sound to /s/, /t/, /p/, /c/, /h/, /r/, /m/, /d/, /g/, /l/, /f/ and /b/. For example, say /ff/ not /fuh/ and /sss/ not /suh/.

Bess has made a test.

The best gift in the land
will win **her** hand.

"**I** must win," **said** Jack.

But Jack **does** not **have** much,
just his dog Sam.

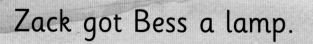

Zack got Bess a lamp.

"It is dull!" said Bess.

Russ got Bess a silk quilt.

"It is dull!" said Bess.

Max got Bess a red belt.

"It is dull!" said Bess.

Jack felt sad.
He had no gift for Bess.

But Sam can help.

Sam ran off fast.

Jump! Sam sat on Bess.

Bess got a lick. Sam got a pat.

"A pet is the best gift yet!"
said Bess.

"Jack wins **my** hand."

OVER **48** TITLES IN SIX LEVELS
Betty Franchi recommends...

Other titles to enjoy from Level 1

I love reading phonics — **Clint and Grant Play I-Spy**
978 1 84898 752 4

I love reading phonics — **A Dragon in the Sandbox**
978 1 84898 754 8

I love reading phonics — **Bret and Grandma's Trip!**
978 1 84898 751 7

Some titles from Level 2

I love reading phonics — **Wish Fish**
978 1 84898 755 5

I love reading phonics — **Chuck and Duck**
978 1 84898 756 2

I love reading phonics — **Pink Bunny**
978 1 84898 760 9

I love reading phonics — **Let's go to the Swings**
978 1 84898 759 3

Some titles from Level 3

I love reading phonics — **Bart's Go-Cart**
978 1 84898 768 5

I love reading phonics — **Queen Ella's Feet**
978 1 84898 764 7

I love reading phonics — **Puff Flies**
978 1 84898 765 4

I love reading phonics — **The Pop Duet**
978 1 84898 767 8

An Hachette Company
First Published in the United States by TickTock, an imprint of Octopus Publishing Group.
www.octopusbooksusa.com

Copyright © Octopus Publishing Group Ltd 2013

Distributed in the US by
Hachette Book Group USA
237 Park Avenue, New York NY 10017, USA

Distributed in Canada by
Canadian Manda Group
165 Dufferin Street, Toronto, Ontario, Canada M6K 3H6

ISBN 978 1 84898 750 0

Printed and bound in China
10 9 8 7 6 5 4 3 2 1